Little Red Riding Hood

Fairy Tale Treasury

Adapted by
Jane Jerrard

Illustrated by
Susan Spellman

Publications International, Ltd.

A long time ago, there was a great forest. A little girl lived with her mother in a tiny village at the edge of the forest.

The girl's grandmother, who loved her more than kittens love mischief, had made her a beautiful red velvet riding cloak. The girl wore the hooded cloak all the time, and so she came to be called Little Red Riding Hood.

One day, Little Red Riding Hood's mother asked her to take a basket of food to her grandmother, who was sick. Little Red Riding Hood set out right away. She promised to go straight to her grandmother's.

Though her grandmother's house was deep in the forest, Little Red Riding Hood knew which path to take, and she was not a bit afraid to walk by herself. She was not even afraid when she met a wolf that day!

Now the wolf, as you probably know, was a wicked animal, and not to be trusted. But he was very polite to Little Red Riding Hood.

She happily answered all his questions. She even told him where her grandmother lived and how to get there! And all the time that wicked wolf was thinking about how much he'd like to eat the little girl and her basket of food.

As the wolf walked with Little Red Riding Hood, he told her, "It's such a lovely day! You should enjoy yourself and pick some flowers!" Little Red Riding Hood thought that the wolf was right.

So she left the path and started to gather the prettiest flowers she could find. She daydreamed a little as she searched, and she forgot about her promise to go straight to her grandmother's house.

Meanwhile, the wolf ran straight to Grandmother's house, lickety-split. There he knocked gently on the door. He disguised his voice and said he was Little Red Riding Hood. When she saw the wolf come in, poor Grandmother jumped right out of bed, only to faint from fright!

The wolf only wanted to eat Little Red Riding Hood, so he disguised himself with Grandmother's cap and nightgown and jumped into her bed.

When Little Red Riding Hood remembered her sick grandmother, she rushed to the little house. There, she found the door wide open.

"Grandmother, are you home?" she called timidly, peeking in the door.

She saw her grandmother lying in bed, with her lacy cap pulled low and the covers pulled up to her chin.

"**M**y, Grandmother, what big ears you have!" she said.

"The better to hear you with, my dear," said the wolf in a high voice.

"What big eyes you have, Grandmother!" said Little Red Riding Hood.

"The better to see you with."

"But, Grandmother, what big teeth you have!"

"The better to EAT you with!"

And with that, the wolf jumped out of the bed to gobble up Little Red Riding Hood! But she was too quick for that wolf. She jumped out of his reach and ran straight out the open door. Luckily, the wild wolf was not used to wearing nightgowns and he had a hard time chasing her.

"Help! Help! A wolf!" cried Little Red Riding Hood.

Now, a hunter had been after that wicked wolf for days, and had followed him right up to Grandmother's house. When the wolf leaped out the door, the hunter shot him dead, quick as a wink.

Little Red Riding Hood and the hunter went inside and woke poor Grandmother. Then the three shared a feast from the basket of good things to eat. And from that day on, Little Red Riding Hood always obeyed her mother!